Iran

by Robin S. Doak

Content Adviser: Beatrice Manz,
Associate Professor of History, Tufts University

Reading Adviser: Dr. Linda D. Labbo,
Department of Reading Education, College of Education,
The University of Georgia

COMPASS POINT BOOKS
MINNEAPOLIS, MINNESOTA

FIRST REPORTS

Compass Point Books
3109 West 50th Street, #115
Minneapolis, MN 55410

Visit Compass Point Books on the Internet at *www.compasspointbooks.com*
or e-mail your request to *custserv@compasspointbooks.com*

On the cover: Friday Mosque in Yazd, Iran

Photographs ©: Corbis, cover; Cory Langley, 4, 24, 26, 27, 28, 29, 30, 32, 33, 34, 39; John Elk III, 7, 31, 36, 41; Ken Lucas/Visuals Unlimited, 8; North Wind Picture Archives, 9, 13; Bettmann/Corbis, 10, 14, 15, 17, 18; SEF/Art Resource, 11; Maryam Amouzegar/Corbis, 19; Francoise de Mulder/Corbis, 20; ATTA KENARE/AFP/Getty Images, 21; V&A/Art Resource, 23; Reuters NewMedia Inc./Corbis, 25; Wolfgang Kaehler/www.wkaehlerphoto.com, 35; David Turnley/Corbis, 37; Scott Peterson/Liaison/Getty Images, 38; Earl & Nazima Kowall/Corbis, 40; Dave Bartruff/Corbis, 42–43.

Editor: Patricia Stockland
Photo Researcher: Marcie C. Spence
Designer/Page Production: Bradfordesign, Inc./Biner Design
Cartographer: XNR Productions, Inc.

Library of Congress Cataloging-in-Publication Data
Doak, Robin S. (Robin Santos), 1963–
    Iran / by Robin Doak.
        p. cm. — (First reports)
    Summary: Introduces the geography, history, culture, and people of Iran, a large, rugged country in southwestern Asia.
    Includes bibliographical references and index.
    ISBN 0-7565-0581-X
    1. Iran—Juvenile literature. [1. Iran.] I. Title. II. Series.
    DS254.75.D63 2004
    955—dc22   2003014432

Table of Contents

*NOTE: In this book, words that are defined in the glossary are in **bold** the first time they appear in the text.*

Salam!

▲ Welcome to Iran!

"*Salam!*" In Iran, this is the way to say "hello." Iran is
a country in the Middle East.

Iran is bordered on the north by Armenia,
Azerbaijan, Turkmenistan, and the Caspian Sea. The

▲ Map of Iran

Persian Gulf and the Gulf of Oman border the country

on the south. To the west of Iran lie Turkey and Iraq.

Afghanistan and Pakistan are the nation's neighbors to

the east. Iran is a large country. It is slightly bigger than the state of Alaska in the United States.

Part of Iran is made up of rugged mountain ranges. The tallest peak in the country is Mount Damavand. It is more than 18,600 feet (5,673 meters) tall. Low, level plains are found along the Caspian Sea and in the western part of the nation. Most of Iran is elevated **plateau.**

Iran's climate is mostly dry. Summers are very hot. In the winter, regions in the north become very cold. Winters in the southern parts of Iran are much warmer. Because Iran is a dry country, most farming needs **irrigation.** The area between the Elburz Mountains and the Caspian Sea is different, though. Trees and rice grow here. This region receives more water than the rest of the country.

There are many different types of plants and animals in Iran. Most of the forests in the country were destroyed a long time ago. However, oak, elm, ash,

▲ *Mount Damavand is the tallest mountain in Iran.*

and walnut trees still grow wild in the mountains. In the desert, cacti and other strong plants manage to survive. Animals found in Iran include tigers, leopards, hyenas, deer, bears, and foxes, as well as other smaller wildlife.

The Caspian Sea is known for its many different types of fish. One type is the sturgeon. It is an ancient kind of fish that is in danger of dying out from pollution and overfishing. Sturgeon eggs are called caviar. Iran's caviar is famous throughout the world.

▲ *If the ancient sturgeon died out, there would be no more left on Earth.*

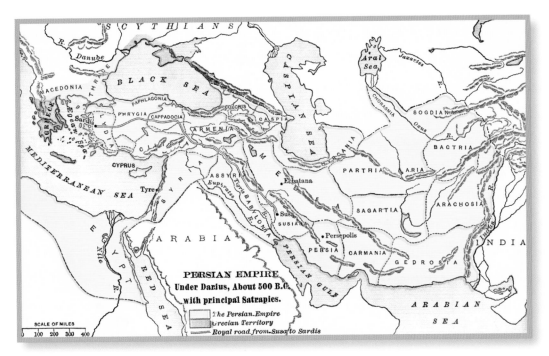

Map labels: SCYTHIANS, R. Danube, BLACK SEA, CASPIAN SEA, Aral Sea, Jaxartes, MACEDONIA, THRACE, PAPHLAGONIA, GREECE, PHRYGIA, CAPPADOCIA, COLCHIS, CASPIA, CHORASMIA, SOGDIANA, Oxus R., ARMENIA, BACTRIA, MEDIA, CYPRUS, Sardis, LYDIA, CILICIA, HYRCANIA, PARTHIA, ARIA, ASSYRIA, Euphrates, Tigris, Ecbatana, Tyre, SYRIA, BABYLONIA, Susa, SUSIANA, SAGARTIA, ARACHOSIA, MEDITERRANEAN SEA, ARABIA, Persepolis, PERSIA, CARMANIA, GEDROSIA, INDIA, EGYPT, Nile R., RED SEA, PERSIAN GULF, ARABIAN SEA

PERSIAN EMPIRE
Under Darius, About 500 B.C.
with principal Satrapies.
The Persian Empire
Grecian Territory
Royal road from Susa to Sardis

SCALE OF MILES
0 100 200 300 400

▲ This map of ancient Persia shows how much area the empire ruled, including all the land that is now Iran.

Iran's history stretches back thousands of years. In the earliest days, Iran was the center of a great empire called the Persian Empire. For many years, the Persian Empire was the strongest in the ancient world. It controlled Mesopotamia, Egypt, and parts

▲ *A Greek coin of Alexander the Great*

of Greece. There was no strict rule during this time, and the different regions kept their own gods and traditions. Zoroastrianism was a common religion that had two gods, one for good and one for evil.

In 334 B.C., Alexander the Great conquered the Persian Empire. Alexander brought Greek culture to Persia. This was just the first of many times the region would be attacked by outsiders. The most important attack began in 634 A.D. That year, Arab Muslims invaded Persia. The Persian Empire fell to the Arabs in 651 A.D. with the death of the Persian emperor. The Arabs brought their Islamic religion to the area. Islam eventually replaced Zoroastrianism. People still spoke Persian at this time but began writing it in the easier Arabic alphabet. This is still done today.

In the 1500s, Shah Ismail founded the Safavid **dynasty.** He turned the area into a Shi'ite state. This

▲ *Shah Ismail battles the Uzbek Shibani Khan over who would rule eastern Persia.*

is a different type of Islam from what most of the world's Muslims now follow. Ismail's father, who was part of a religious **order,** had been killed in tribal fighting when Ismail was 7. Some of his father's followers hid him in the mountains. At the age of 12, Ismail set out to get even for his father's death by gathering tribes to follow his leadership. He also claimed to be semidivine, or like a god. Within a year, he had conquered the entire area and claimed the title of king, or shah. He also made all of the Muslims in the area change to Shi'ism. Kings known as shahs ruled the empire for the next 400 years.

By the 19th century, Persia was very poor compared to Europe. The government was weak. The nation wanted to modernize, so students were sent to study in Europe. The Europeans controlled many goods made in Persia and had a stronger military. During this time, different shahs tried to make deals

▲ *Shahs, such as Fath 'Ali, ruled Ismail's empire for 400 years.*

with the Europeans, but they ended up owing the Europeans a lot of money. These problems and changes eventually led to the Constitutional Revolution.

The 20th Century

For Iran, the 20th century was one of conflict. In the early 1900s, the people of Persia rebelled against the shahs of the Qajar dynasty during the Constitutional Revolution. Some people were fighting to get a stronger parliament, which is a group of elected law-makers. They also wanted a **constitution** that limited the shah's power. The Qajar dynasty stayed in power, but Persians got more rights and greater freedom.

▲ *Reza Khan (center) with a group of officers*

▲ *The 1926 coronation, or crowning, of Reza Khan, the first shah of the Pahlavi dynasty*

The Pahlavi dynasty started in 1925. The shahs of this dynasty had a constitution, but they still controlled the government and the people. In 1935, Reza Khan, the first shah of the Pahlavi dynasty, changed the name of the country from Persia to Iran. New laws were forced on the people that **westernized** their clothing and **secularized** their society. The new dynasty also put a lot of money into the military. This was done mainly to control people within the nation rather than protect them.

Iranians were again unhappy with their shah by the late 1970s. Shah Mohammad Reza Pahlavi had created a one-party government. This kept anyone from opposing his ideas. He used secret police to control people who tried to speak out against him. He also changed the Muslim calendar to one based on the Persian Empire. This upset people who used the Muslim calendar for religious purposes. Some who opposed the shah were writers, lawyers, and Muslim religious leaders. They felt the shah was moving away from Islam and its traditional beliefs.

In 1979, the shah was forced out of Iran. A religious leader named Ayatollah Ruhollah Khomeini took control of the government. *Ayatollah* is the title given to the most important Muslim leaders.

▲ Followers greet Ayatollah Khomeini in 1979.

Under the shah, Iran and the United States enjoyed good relations. The United States had supported the shah. After the revolution, however, everything changed. In November 1979, angry college students in Iran

▲ *A few Islamic guards and TV crews stand outside the U.S. embassy building during the hostage crisis.*

captured the U.S. **embassy** building in Tehran. The students created a major hostage crisis when they held 52 Americans captive for 444 days. The Americans were finally released in January 1981.

During the hostage crisis, the United States broke off relations with Iran. Relations between the two countries are still tense today. The United States bans most trade with Iran.

After the Revolution

After Khomeini was in power, Iran became an Islamic republic. This means that Shi'ite Islam is the official religion of the country. Iran has a functioning democracy with an elected president and parliament. However, that is only one part of the government. The other side

is the supreme *faqih*, or supreme religious leader, who is ruler for life. He has the final say on what the religious laws will be. The two parts of government often have very different views and goals for the nation.

◄ *President Khatami addresses the parliament.*

▲ *Iraqi soldiers invade Iran.*

Khomeini named himself the country's first supreme faqih. Khomeini's government passed many strict laws. These laws banned anything that was considered non-Islamic. For example, alcohol, certain types of music, and some textbooks were outlawed. Some who opposed Khomeini were killed.

In 1980, Saddam Hussein led Iraq in an invasion of Iran. The two countries fought over water rights and control of oil-rich land. Thousands of people lost their lives during the bloody war. The war ended in 1988 with no real winner. Iran and Iraq still disagree over borders between the two countries.

Ayatollah Khomeini died in 1989. Today, Iran's faqih is Ayatollah Ali Hoseini-Khamenei. In recent years, students and the general public have been calling for greater freedom. While some laws have been loosened, others have not. Those who speak out against the government are often thrown in jail.

▲ *Outside Tehran University in 2003, Iranian students seeking more freedom and greater democracy hold a demonstration.*

The Muslim Religion

The national religion of Iran is Shi'a Islam. Nine out of every 10 Iranians follow this religion. Followers are often called Shi'ites. Islam, Christianity, and Judaism all share the same story of creation, with Adam and Eve, and believe in the history of Abraham, Moses, and David.

Muslims follow a book called the Koran. They believe it includes the teachings of God, which were revealed to Muhammad. He was a prophet who lived from around 570 A.D. to 632 A.D. Muslims believe that Jesus was also a prophet. Unlike Christians, however, they do not believe he is the Son of God.

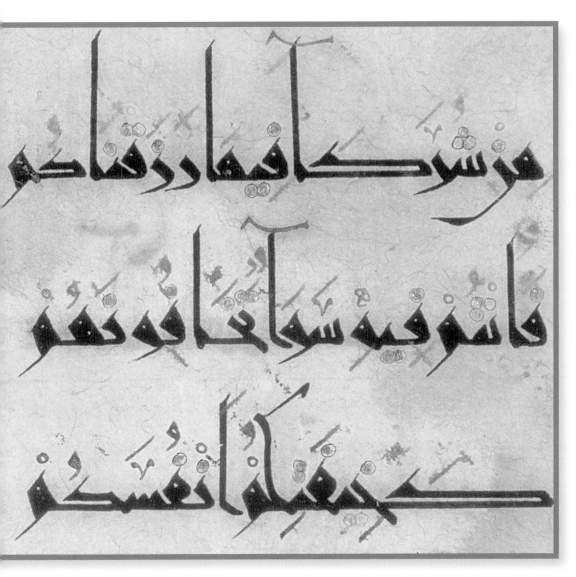

▲ *This page of the Koran dates from the 11th century. The Koran
and its teachings are very important to Muslims.*

▲ *Mosques are places of worship.*

Mosques are places where Muslims go to worship. On Fridays, Muslims gather together to pray at the mosque. A curtain separates men and women from one another.

Pilgrimages are an important part of the Muslim religion. These are trips people take to scared places. Each year, millions of people visit the shrines of ancient Islamic leaders. These shrines are located throughout Iran and the neighboring country of Saudi Arabia.

▲ *A symbolic attacker pretends to scare Iranian schoolchildren during an Ashura ceremony. Ashura is part of the Muharram celebration.*

One of the holiest shrines in Iran is in Mashad. The shrine contains a hospital, several mosques, and a museum.

Shi'a Muslims celebrate several holy periods. One of the most important is during Muharram, the first month of the year. During the first 10 days of the month, people mourn the death of Muhammad's grandson with religious plays and ceremonies. Another important time for all Muslims is Ramadan, a month of fasting.

A much smaller number of people in Iran are Sunni Muslims. Sunni Islam is the religion practiced by most Muslims around the world. Smaller groups of people in Iran include Baha'is, Christians, and Jews.

25

Life in Iran

▲ *Small villages can be found throughout rural Iran.*

Iran is home to more than 66 million people. More than half are Persian. Other groups of people living in Iran include Kurds, Arabs, Armenians, and Turks. Many of these groups live in tribes scattered throughout rural Iran.

Several different languages are spoken in Iran. The most common language is Persian, or Farsi. More than half the nation's people speak Persian. Other groups speak their own language. Visitors might hear Kurdish in some areas and Turkish in other places.

▲ Street signs are often posted in more than one language.

In Iran, women are not treated the same as men. The Islamic republic limits women's actions in public, and men and women must be separated. Men do not shake women's hands in public. Women cannot go to some sporting events. Until they reach college, they must attend separate schools. However, women do have a right to education and jobs.

▲ *Women wearing the chador, which is often black*

Women are required to cover their heads and wear long, shapeless clothes in public. Some wear the *chador*, a long garment that covers most of the body. Only the hands and face are visible. The rights of women are a serious issue in Iran today.

People who break the rules or speak out against the government risk punishment. They could be whipped or put into prison.

More than half of Iran's population live in cities. Iran's capital and largest city is Tehran. It is located in the northern part of the nation, near the Caspian Sea. Tehran is more than 700 years old, but it only became a crowded, bustling city during the past 100 years. It is very polluted.

Another large city is Mashhad. It is important because of its shrines and its manufacturing.

▲ *Tehran, Iran's largest city*

Carpets, textiles, and other goods are made here. Other big cities in Iran include Isfahan, Tabriz, and Shiraz. These cities are also important religious, cultural, and manufacturing centers.

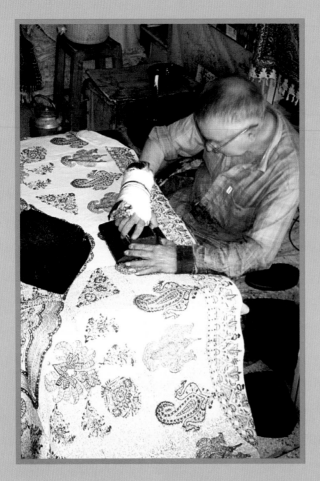
▲ *A man works on textiles in Isfahan.*

Every city or town in Iran has its own bazaar. The bazaar is a covered street or alley lined with shops. It is often a wonderful, colorful place full of sounds, smells, and activity. Here, people can buy food, clothes, and other items. In big cities, the bazaar may stretch over many streets. It may include hundreds of shops, as well as restaurants, baths, gardens, and schools.

▲ *Fruits and vegetables fill part of the Yazd bazaar.*

Iran's cities continue to grow. Young men and women from the countryside often leave home to move to the city. They are more likely to find work there.

Thousands of small villages are scattered throughout Iran. Some are tiny, made up of just a few families. Others are the size of small towns, with thousands of residents.

▲ *Farming is a way of life for most villagers.*

Most villagers make their living through farming. About half of all villagers own land for farming. Many who don't own land work as farm laborers. Others are merchants, carpenters, shoe makers, blacksmiths, and other tradespeople.

Some Iranians are nomads. These are people who move from place to place for their animals' food. Most nomads in Iran are sheep and goat herders. In the summer, the nomadic tribes move into the mountains where there is more grass available for the animals. In the winter, they move back to the plains.

Nomads trade with local villagers for items they need. Nomadic tribes have animals, hides, wool, and dairy goods. They trade these goods for manufactured or agricultural items.

▲ *Nomads often trade animals and animal products for manufactured goods.*

Arts and Culture

Iran has a long history of amazing arts and crafts. Persian music, literature, and architecture date from ancient times and are famous. Beautiful Persian rugs are prized throughout the world. These brightly colored works of art have patterns and pictures of flowers, birds, and animals.

Calligraphy is the art of handwriting. Iranian artists are some of the best calligraphers in the world. Calligraphy is

▲ Persian rugs are made by hand.

used in texts and as decoration on mosques. Other Iranian arts include metalworking, engraving, painting, textiles, and pottery.

Iranian architecture is some of the most amazing to be found. Many ancient and historic sites still stand throughout the country. One of the most famous is Shah Mosque in Isfahan.

▲ *Colorful tiles cover the huge Shah Mosque in Isfahan.*

▲ *Designs stand out from their flat background in these reliefs at Persepolis.*

Another famous site in Iran is the ancient ruins of Persepolis. Begun in 512 B.C., Persepolis was the palace of Persian kings. The city was burned to the ground by Alexander the Great in 331 B.C. Visitors can still see the ancient columns, reliefs, and arches that remain.

Manners are another part of Iranian culture. This formal Persian politeness is called *ta'rof*. A person does not accept anything, including food, until the third time it is offered. If someone is visiting and wants to leave, they ask permission to go.

Education in Iran

Children in Iran begin school when they are 6 years old. Girls and boys go to separate schools. These schools are free and open to all children. All Iranian students must complete the first five grades of school. They study reading, writing, arts, mathematics, social studies, and the Koran.

▲ Girls at an Islamic school

Students may continue their studies through secondary school and high school. After students graduate from high school, they may choose to attend one of Iran's universities. The largest university is in Tehran. Some students choose to travel to other countries to study.

Madraseh are special schools where men can go to learn more about their religion. Most students here study for at least seven years to become a *mullah,* or religious scholar. They may be preachers, judges, or teachers.

▲ *Students such as these Islamic clerics must attend madraseh to become religious scholars.*

Food in Iran

▲ *Spices add a great variety of flavors to Iranian foods.*

▲ *Schoolboys holding nan-e lavash*

There is a great variety of foods and flavors in Iran. Herbs like mint, dill, and parsley are used to make soups, meats, and vegetables delicious.

The main food in Iran is rice. It is served in many different ways. Rice can be stuffed into vegetables or mixed with meat, chicken, fruit, or nuts. Fruit in Iran is also very good and very popular.

Bread is another important food. One type of bread that is enjoyed is *nan-e lavash.* It is a thin bread often eaten for breakfast.

Stews, soups, yogurt dips, and kabobs are all favorite dishes in Iran. A kabob is chicken, lamb, or other meat served on a skewer.

Iranians love sweets. Pastries flavored with honey, cinnamon, and rose water are popular. Tea, called *chai,* is the most popular drink. It is sweetened with many cubes of sugar. Usually, a person puts the sugar cube in his or her mouth and drinks the tea through the cube.

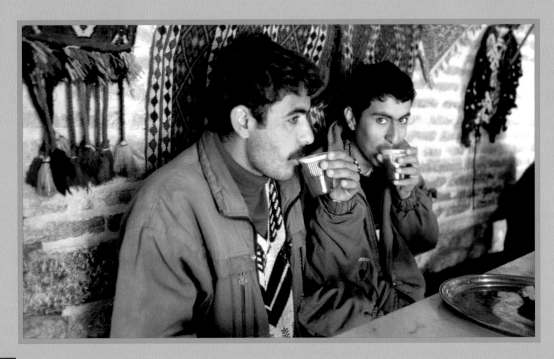

▲ *Sweet tea is very popular in Iran.*

Iran Today

▲ *Oil is very important to Iran.*

Iran's most important industry is oil, which is controlled by the government. The country is one of the top oil-producing nations in the world. Nearly 9,000 miles (14,400 kilometers) of pipelines are used to send oil, petroleum, and natural gas from around the country to port cities on the Persian Gulf. The nation's chief port is Abadan. Each year, millions of tons of oil are shipped from the ports to countries around the world.

Iran's factories make textiles, cement, processed foods, and metals. Iran is rich in mineral resources, too. Important minerals found in Iran include zinc, coal, copper, iron, and lead.

Before the 1970s, Iran was mostly a farming country. In villages throughout Iran, people still make their living by farming. Iranian farmers grow wheat, rice, sugar beets, fruits, and nuts. Dairy products and wool contribute to the economy as well.

Iran is a country rich not only in minerals but also in culture and history. Iranians are struggling toward more equality and a better life for all citizens. At the same time, they are keeping their colorful traditions alive.

▲ *A metal artisan at work*

Glossary

constitution—a document describing the government and basic rules of a country

dynasty—a sequence, or series, of rulers from the same family

embassy—a building in one country where the representatives of another country work

irrigation—a way of bringing water to fields through canals or ditches

order—people in a group who live under the same rules

plateau—high, flat ground

secularized—something changed from religious use to civil use

westernized—to give western qualities to something, especially like those of some European and North American countries

Did You Know?

- Powerful earthquakes are quite common in Iran. In 1990, a serious earthquake in western Iran killed more than 40,000 people.

- Soccer is the favorite sport in Iran. Wrestling and basketball are also popular.

- Iran uses three different calendars: a Persian calendar based on the sun, an Islamic calendar, and a Gregorian calendar. (The Gregorian calendar is the one that is used in the United States.)

Official name: *Jomhuri-ye Eslami-ye Iran* (Islamic Republic of Iran)

Capital: Tehran

Official language: Persian, or Farsi

National song: *Sorood-e-Jomhoori-e-Islami* (Anthem of the Islamic Republic of Iran)

Area: 636,300 square miles (1,654,380 square km)

Highest point: Mount Damavand, 18,602 feet (5,674 m) above sea level

Lowest point: Caspian Sea, 92 feet (28 m) below sea level

Population: 66,622,704 (2002 estimate)

Heads of state: Faqih (supreme religious leader) and President

Money: Rial

Important Dates

550 B.C.	The first Persian Empire is founded.
651 A.D.	Persia is conquered by Muslim Arabs, and Islam is introduced.
1500	The Safavids establish themselves in Persia, causing the conversion to Shi'ism.
1906–1911	The Constitutional Revolution tries to establish a stronger elected parliament with a less powerful shah.
1925	The Pahlavi dynasty begins.
1935	Persia becomes known as Iran.
1979	The last shah is forced out of power. Ayatollah Khomeini assumes leadership of Iran.
1980	An eight-year war with Iraq begins.
1981	American hostages are released from Iran after 444 days in captivity.
1989	Ayatollah Khomeini dies.
2003	Shirin Ebadi, the first female Iranian judge, wins the Nobel Peace Prize.

Want to Know More?

At the Library

Bader, Philip, and Patricia Moritz. *Dropping In on Iran.* Vero Beach,
    Fla.: Rourke Book Company, 2002.
Schemenauer, Elma. *Iran.* Chanhassen, Minn.: Child's World, 2000.
Wagner, Heather Lehr, and Akbar Ahmed. *Iran.* Philadelphia: Chelsea
    House, 2002.

On the Web

For more information on Iran, use FactHound
to track down Web sites related to this book.

1. Go to *www.compasspointbooks.com/facthound*
2. Type in this book ID: 075650581X
3. Click on the *Fetch It* button.

Your trusty FactHound will fetch the best Web sites for you!

Through the Mail

National Iranian American Council
2451 18th St. N.W., 2nd Floor
Washington, DC 20009
202/518-6187
info@niacouncil.org
For more information on Iranian American activities, contributions,
and history

On the Road

The Foundation for Iranian Studies
4343 Montgomery Ave.
Bethesda, MD 20814
301/657-1990
fis@fis-iran.org
To visit a library of Iranian and Persian history, culture, life, and arts

Index

About the Author

Robin S. Doak has been writing for children for more than 14 years. A former editor of Weekly Reader and U*S*Kids magazine, Ms. Doak has authored fun and educational materials for kids of all ages. Some of her work includes biographies of explorers such as Henry Hudson and John Smith, as well as other titles in this series. Ms. Doak is a past winner of the Educational Press Association of America Distinguished Achievement Award. She lives with her husband and three children in central Connecticut.